THE MAKING OF A ROCK

A Novella

By: Tylie Vaughan Eaves

Vertū Publishing, 2020

A Component of Vertū Marketing, LLC

VERTŪ PUBLISHING
A Component of Vertū Marketing LLC
www.vertu-marketing.com

Ordering Information:
Quantity sales. Special discounts are available on quantity purchases by corporations, associations, and others. For details, contact the publisher at the address above.
Orders by U.S. trade bookstores and wholesalers.
Please contact: Tel: (866) 779-0795.

Printed in the United States of America
ISBN 978-1-7350078-0-9

THIS IS A WORK OF FICTION

Written with a reason; written to inspire.

The Making of a Rock

A Fictional First-Person Account of the Passion, Through the Eyes of an Unlikely Disciple

The light of the moon washed over every surface in sight, like a shower of goat's milk under the night sky. Light bounced off the homes of my sleeping neighbors in a way that cast eerie shadows onto the street. Unable to sleep, I stood staring up at the stars, filling my lungs with the night air. As I contemplated returning to my bedchamber, I heard the sound of footsteps approaching in a rapid clamour from the west. I turned to see a man running straight toward me, fleeing the courtyard outside The House of Annas. In the distance, I could see the warmth of torches and lamplight dancing behind the courtyard walls – too much light for the hour! The man gasped for air as he ran, and he ran like he was being chased. I found myself instantly frightened. What had this man done?

My breath caught in my chest as I watched him pass. I stayed in the shadows as I turned my eyes back toward the west, expecting guards or a mob to follow, but no one else approached. The dust from the ground floated into the air like a fine mist in the moonlight as I watched the man fall to his knees. His shoulders shook violently as he wept aloud, wailing with a bitterness unlike anything I'd ever heard before. He fell forward onto his face, pressing his forehead into the dirt as he cried out. Even from a distance, I could see the glistening of tears that stained his face, falling freely from his eyes and streaking the dust that now covered his body in a thin veil. I felt a pain in the pit of my stomach; the sight of him made me ache. He wore brokenness like a cloak and the pain in his cry was so palpable I wanted to turn away – but I could not.

With apprehension, I slowly made my way toward him. My hands trembled as I reached down to touch his shoulder. As soon as my fingers grazed his tunic, he jumped as if I'd struck him. He looked up at me with a wide-eyed fear, gasping for breath. He reminded me of a frightened child – but something about his gaze pierced my heart and something inside me compelled me to comfort him. His face was dark, as though he'd spent his days working in the sun, and though his eyes were consumed with fear, they carried a certain kindness I could not mistake. "Sir, are you alright?" I asked in earnest, but I was sorely unprepared for his response.

"I denied him!" he cried out. I had no idea what he meant.

"I'm sorry, what?"

I watched him cover his face with both hands as he repeated in a whisper, "I denied him." The tone in his speech was thick with grief, but I somehow recognized the sound of his voice. I was certain this man had to be one of the twelve followers of the Galilean, or was it the Nazarene? I had heard him called by both names, and I wasn't sure which to embrace. The whole of Jerusalem had been talking about the "so called" prophet who had performed miracles. My brother and his wife had gone so far as to meet him at the city gates and to lay palm fronds at his feet just days prior. I opened my mouth to speak again, but the words wouldn't come. Instead, I reached down to help the weeping man to his feet. "The rooster," he said, as he peered at me through wet, bloodshot eyes. Again, I wanted to speak but could say nothing. Had he gone mad? A rooster?

Suddenly, lamplight illuminated a nearby window and the man quickly wiped his eyes. I was startled along with him. He took the sash from around his waist and draped it over his head, wrapping a free end over his face. He nodded his thanks and quickly turned to flee, but instead of returning to my own home, I followed closely behind him. It was as if I had no control over my own feet. Something deep inside me urged me onward. He turned toward me, likely to shoo me away, but he didn't speak. I heard the sound of footsteps nearby and, without even thinking, I pulled the man into the shadows between two buildings to conceal his presence. I leaned into the street, waiting for the foreboding presence to pass. I turned to face the man, and when his eyes met mine, he stared into me with a powerful intensity. Then, a note of both gratitude and understanding formed in his expression. He nodded slightly and turned his back again. I can't explain it, but I felt as though he fully understood my inability to turn away.

I followed closely behind him. We moved with speed, but neither of us spoke a word. He wanted to stay in the shadows, and though I didn't know why, I kept to the shadows as well. A cloud blotted out the moon for a short while, engulfing the path in darkness as we turned a corner and headed toward a house in the distance. The inkiness of the night wavered as the cloud relented, allowing the moon's light to fill the early morning sky once again. As we arrived to the house, I could see a single sliver of lamplight gleaming from beneath the batten of a lone upper window. The man reached out to check the gate, but it was barred. He looked around nervously as he began to knock. He knocked twice, and then paused to look around again. His obvious discomfort made me anxious as well, though I had yet to understand why. As he checked our surroundings yet another time, I saw a dark shadow block the sliver of lamplight above our heads.

A few moments later, there was a noise beyond the gate. It opened slightly at first, and then the gap widened enough for me to see the face of another man. "Peter!" The other man's voice was a loud whisper and a symphony of relief as he threw his arms around my newly acquired companion. As they embraced, I focused on committing Peter's name to memory. "I was worried the guards had shackled you," the other man said. I could see the hesitation in his eyes as he looked at Peter, then to me, and then back to Peter again. Peter laid a hand on the man's shoulder and nodded, and the man immediately gave me a reluctant greeting. I followed them inside. The man seemed to take extra care with barring the gate and, as Peter led the way, I found myself wondering briefly if these holy men weren't what they seemed. Why the secrecy? What were we hiding from?

Once inside, I could feel a palpable tension in the room. The air was stuffy, and as I looked about, I took note of the fact that every window was battened down. I looked around to see yet more men with tired, tearstained cheeks, and I watched the lamplight bounce off their pained faces as their confusion at my presence demanded an explanation. It was an unexpected collection of faces. One man had forearms like tree limbs, strong and sinewy. Another had a slim build and wore a fine tunic. He reminded me of the men one might find at a tax table. Again, Peter only nodded. It became evident to me that Peter was somehow chief among them, a leader of sorts.

No one spoke. The quiet in the room was thicker than silence, heavier somehow. It was almost as though I had tufts of lamb's wool in my ears. Within minutes, a fair looking woman in a worn blue stola emerged from the stairway with a basket of warm bread and a bowl of dates. She, too, had clearly spent the evening in tears. She quietly placed the food on a small table by the lantern and turned to go, as no one seemed interested in eating. I was struck by her beauty. She bore refined features and carried herself modestly. The woman paused in front of Peter, looked into his eyes, and bowed her head deeply as if she were in great pain. Peter raised his hand and placed it gently on the back of her head for just a moment. She stood there crying for several minutes before she wiped her eyes with the free end of the tichel that neatly covered her hair, and then she left as suddenly as she had appeared.

No sooner did she leave our sight than we heard knocking at the gate once again. Every man in the room jumped in to ready positions, as though they expected the worst. I felt fear welling inside me as I looked toward Peter, who glanced at me with a knowing expression. Though his weeping had subsided, his face appeared sunken and tired. His heavy heart was visible in every pore. He moved quickly to the window and I followed, we both peered out through the tiny crack below the batten. "It's alright," he said as he turned back toward the room. I could feel the relief in the air as the men collectively abandoned their ready positions. "James," Peter continued, "it looks to be John. Go down and let him in." The man who had greeted Peter and I just moments before again rose to his feet and efficiently made his way down the stairs. Once again, I found myself claiming a moment to commit names to memory.

I turned my gaze back to the man at the gate they called John. His breath was heaving. He panted as though he'd run all the way from Damascus. I squinted against the still-looming dark as James threw his arms around John, embracing him with the same fervor as Peter before him. The two shared a brief exchange. I struggled to hear them, but I could only make out a few words: Sanhedrin, Pilate, and dawn. I could instantly feel my heartbeat in my ears. What had I walked into? The Sanhedrin? Had I made a grave mistake?

When James and John were safely back inside, John was still breathing heavily. The other men sat up, riveted by his presence. "Tell them," James said emphatically. They each waited with baited breath to hear what John might say. The woman returned again and presented John with a water cup. He took the craft and drank eagerly and quickly with large gulps. The entire room waited in profound anticipation.

"Oh, dear Mary, thank you," John said breathlessly, as he wiped the excess moisture from his lips with the back of his hand. Another name to remember. This time Mary stayed. She reached for John's cup as he began to speak. "The Sanhedrin have condemned him. He will go on trial before Pilate at dawn," he spewed the words into the air as though they tasted badly in his mouth.

"So quickly?" Peter spit out his words in return. He seemed dismayed. Truly, in all my years, I'd never heard of another trial that had been conducted so suddenly, and in the wee hours of the morning no less – it all seemed somehow evil. "He told us all this *must* happen. We all heard him." Peter continued, "We watched him give himself over to the guards. He could have stopped it if he'd chosen to. And in the garden, he told us not to fight back, but how can we simply stand by and do nothing?" He hung his head and grabbed onto his own hair so fiercely that I feared he may pull it out.

"What could we do besides get ourselves arrested alongside him?" James added ardently.

Another man jumped to his feet and shouted, "We should fight back!"

"No!" James shouted in return. "You heard him in the garden. All who draw the sword shall die by the sword! Or have you so quickly forgotten the guard's ear?"

The room fell silent for a long while until another man stood, "I can't just sit here. I'm going to the trial."

"You'll be caught," another said.

"No I won't. I will cloak myself and cover my face."

"I'm going too," John added. He spoke to the entire room and said, "We must all cover our faces when we're outside. We will lose the darkness and will be easily found out." He turned to Peter, "Are you coming?"

Peter stood silently, frozen in place. I could practically see the thoughts running through his mind. I could hear the sound of his voice echoing in my head, "I denied him." He seemed shackled by shame. But after meeting these men and witnessing how they looked to Peter for leadership, I hoped his secret would remain inviolate and that no one else would ever find out about his painful confession there in the road. As I watched Peter wrestle with the consequences of his choices, it dawned on me that I had never met this rabbi, but I had heard the stories. Everyone had. And if these men were any indication of who the Galilean was, then he truly must have been the holiest of rabbis – maybe even a prophet.

As the dawn of a new day began its imminent ascent, Peter, James, John, Mary and I, along with two of the other men, made our way in secret to Antonia Fortress, where the Galilean would stand before Pontius Pilate in what felt like it might be a matter of moments. James and Peter had tried in earnest to keep Mary from making the journey, suggesting that the day's events may be difficult to watch, but Mary could not be dissuaded. "His mother will be there," she said. "I'm sure of it. Someone should be there to help care for her and for his brother."

I thought about her words for a moment. They hung like symbols in my ears. I imagined a mother watching her child stand before the courts. If this rabbi was innocent like they said, then his mother's pain would be magnified tenfold. I prayed I wouldn't meet her. I didn't think I would be able to bear it.

As we traveled, we dared not walk together. Several of the men reiterated the risks of being recognized, so we paired off and allowed lots of space between us. I walked with John and learned through him that James and Peter were brothers. Mary walked just behind them, keeping pace and watching where she stepped, always keeping her eyes downcast, probably to hide the tears that had been flowing freely for hours.

Just before the sun crested the horizon, we stopped outside a vacant storefront just beyond the courtyard at

Antonia, which everyone had come to know as the governor's house. The walls of the court were far too high for us to see anything of note from the street. "Look, we could watch from the rooftop," James whispered. We all followed him up the ladder and kept ourselves behind the cover of the knee-wall as we knelt on the rooftop. "Pull the ladder up behind you," James told one of the men. "It will be safer for us if we do." We watched from the distance as a crowd began to gather around the steps. From our rooftop perch, we began to hear rumblings in the street below. Even the people who were simply going about their daily chores seemed preoccupied by the tension in the air and the suddenness of the holy man's trial. "He's innocent," some would say. "He's a blasphemer," others would claim.

"There he is!" Peter shouted in a whisper, as a bloodied, weary man, bound with chains, was cast forth onto the steps. The man stumbled, but he did not fall. I was transfixed by him, though I struggled to comprehend the scene before me. This man they called The King of the Jews didn't look like a king at all. How could this man be the mighty coming king I'd heard so much about? It didn't seem possible. I looked at Peter, whom I could tell truly believed this man was our Messiah. But when I looked back toward the courtyard, I failed to see the majesty Peter saw. Instead, I saw brokenness. Pilate motioned for his guards, and two men dressed in the garb of the Roman soldier stepped forward and pulled the Galilean up the stairs toward Pilate. Pilate turned quickly, his crimson cape danced in the breeze behind him as he moved. He made his way toward the doorway. The soldiers flanked the Galilean as they continued up the steps and through the grand pillars. We waited.

"I'm going for a closer look," John announced. He slowly slid the ladder down toward the street, keeping his body low behind the wall.

"Be careful, brother," Peter called after him. Mary rose to follow him. "Mary?" Peter asked, as if to question her intent.

"I am not one of the twelve. Perhaps I can get closer than John without risking my freedom."

"She's right," John responded from his position on the ladder.

"So be it," Peter conceded.

I watched as the pair descended and weaved their way into the tapestry of people on the now crowded street. John began to run toward the courtyard, carefully avoiding a handful of the Roman guard as he did so. Mary walked quickly, unencumbered. It seemed like a long while before we saw John's face again, but in actuality, the sun had barely moved in the sky. I moved quickly to help one of his other companions with the ladder, but he waved his hand to stop us. "Pilate has called him innocent! They're taking him before Herod!" He looked over his shoulder in both directions before he continued to speak, "I heard the guards murmuring." He looked around again. "There's no way we'll be able to get close enough, but I'm going to follow the guards as best I can. Perhaps I can call out to him to let him know we are with him."

"Where is Mary?" one of the other men asked, as he looked back toward the crowd in the street.

"I don't know. She stayed with the crowds. She was looking for his mother." As John spoke, another man I didn't recognize ran up behind him. I could tell the others knew him so I let the tension fall from my fists. He was breathing heavily and had panic in his eyes. "They found Judas," he panted. "He hanged himself just outside the city walls!" A hush fell over the group, and I watched a look of remorse spread across Peter's face. There was a strange sense of both grief and justice in the glances shared on the rooftop. I wondered what it meant, but I dared not ask. We could hear the crowd crying out in the distance with renewed intensity, and I turned to watch the man they called rabbi, bound in shackles and flanked by two Roman guards, pressing through the throngs of people making their way toward the courtyard gate.

"I'm going," John announced. He didn't wait for a response and, instead, called over his shoulder to Peter, "I'll be back. Wait here and be safe."

"May God keep you!" Peter called out behind him as John ran into the streets, headed for Herod's palace. I settled back into my spot on the rooftop. The morning light had grown quite bright, so I shaded my eyes with my hand as I watched the crowd continue to grow inside the courtyard. As I watched, unable to look away from the masses, the other men began to share stories, stories unlike anything I'd ever heard before. Of course, I had heard about the Galilean's miracles, everyone had – but I only knew them as they came through the lips of people at the market or at the well. But these men spoke as though they'd seen these things with their own eyes. There was no doubt in their voices – no doubt and no deception. I tore my gaze away from the crowd and looked to Peter.

I mustered the courage to speak for the first time in hours, "Did you really walk on the water?" I whispered. It was as if I'd sounded a horn, suddenly the other men on the rooftop became both aware and abruptly wary of my presence.

"Who are you to ask? Why are you asking questions?" One of the men said sharply. Another reached for a loose stone on the ledge, preparing to pummel me if I answered against his satisfaction. Peter moved in front of me, placing himself between me and my accusers, crouching to remain unseen. He lifted his arms toward his friends disarmingly.

"I trust this man," Peter said. "Though he was a stranger to me, he came to my aid in the street and sacrificed his own safety to help me." As the other men disarmed themselves, Peter answered my original question in a whisper, "Yeshua really did the walking. All I did was cling to him." I felt something akin to excitement building in my heart. I was secretly envious, wishing I had been there to see it with my own eyes. It seemed so impossible, and yet, I believed him.

Once again, we heard John's voice crying out from somewhere among the suddenly boisterous crowd. We all turned to look into the street, scanning the crowd for his face. Peter spotted him, waving his hands over his head to signal his location. He pushed through the throng in the street to cry out to us, "Herod has released him as well! They're taking him back to Pilate!" He turned from us and headed immediately toward the courtyard. We all shifted and moved to ensure we had the most advantageous views, but within mere seconds, Peter was on his feet.

"I'm going. I need to be closer to him. I cannot stay here." He laid hold of the ladder.

I stood to help him. As we lowered it to the street, I spoke, "I'm coming with you. Like Mary, neither am I one of the twelve, perhaps I can help you in some way." Peter bowed his head in thanks. We descended into the multitude. Peter walked closely behind me, keeping his head down, matching my stride step for step. When we passed a member of the Roman guard, he huddled in so close behind me I could feel his heartbeat.

As we pressed in through the gate, the crowd grew especially dense. I caught a glimpse of Mary moving with another woman along the far wall. As I watched, they stepped in behind John and another man I'd yet to meet. The woman with Mary looked torn, as though her heart had been ripped from her chest. I knew immediately that she was the Galilean's mother. My heart seized at the sight of her. "I see John and Mary," I whispered over my shoulder. Peter stayed close behind me. He repeatedly placed his hand on the cloak over his face, as if to ensure his identity was still hidden. We stepped in behind John and Mary and the others. A roar erupted from the crowd. I could see the Galilean shuffling in his shackles toward the stairs. His face appeared more battered than before. A Roman guard shoved him periodically, as if somehow shoving him could lengthen the chains that hindered his stride.

A full company of Roman guards were stationed between the stairs and the crowd, far more than had been present at dawn. Pilate appeared on the stairs before us. He raised a hand toward the crowd and spoke, "Herod has found no cause in this man, nor have I!" Many of the people in the crowd hissed and booed. Pilate raised his hand again. He scanned the crowd with his eyes. He seemed to be sizing up a potential threat. "As you know, each year, I release a prisoner back to you." As he spoke, a trio of guards dragged the man they call Barabbas onto the stairs from somewhere inside the fortress. I knew of Barabbas. He was a notorious robber. He'd been found guilty of insurrection and murder, and he had a much-feared reputation. Just the sight of him made me bristle. His eyes were dark and menacing. His stature was one of intimidation. I found myself clutching my tunic against my chest, and I had to force myself to let it loose. I held my breath as Pilate hushed the crowd.

He questioned the mob, asking which prisoner we'd have him release, the man they call Jesus or the captive Barabbas. From somewhere in the front, we heard the chief priest cry out "Free Barabbas!" As if on cue, the other Pharisees and even much of the crowd began to shout the same.

I don't know what possessed me to do it, but I found words shooting from my lungs all the same, "Jesus!" I cried at the top of my lungs, "Jesus!" Several people in the crowd turned to look at me. I felt suddenly vulnerable, but Peter began to shout with me, as did the rest of our group. Try as we might though, we were no match for the volume of the mob. And then, it happened. I remember it as clearly as I remember my own name. Jesus looked at me. As he stood there on the steps, beaten, exhausted and quiet – he looked right into my eyes ever so briefly. I somehow felt his gaze deep in my soul, and I knew he'd seen me. He'd heard me. And somehow, I felt as though he knew me. I felt renewed – truly, this man must be the Messiah.

"He's seen us," Mary spoke, clutching the hand of Jesus' mother. I could see Jesus lamenting the pain in his own mother's face. The look in his eyes seemed to be one of comfort, despite his own circumstances. Pilate raised his hand again and silenced the crowd. His expression revealed his uncertainty. He asked a second time who the crowd would release, and the response was nearly identical.

Pontius Pilate gestured to his men and they began the arduous process of unshackling the heavily bound Barabbas. "And what then would you have me do with this man they call the Christ?" he shouted as he lifted an open palm toward the rabbi.

The chief priest shouted back in a loud voice, "Crucify him!" He turned toward the crowd, raised both his arms and shouted again, "Crucify him!" The crowd joined in, screaming and spitting and shaking their fists. His mother wailed. Tears cascaded over her cheeks. Mary was all but holding her up. The other man there wrapped an arm around her and held her tightly.

Pilate took a deep breath. I could see his breastplate rise and fall. He raised his eyes toward the balcony where his wife looked on. I can't be certain, but I would almost swear I saw her shake her head and mouth the word "no" in his direction. Pilate turned to the crowd again, and again stated he could find no fault in the man Jesus, but the priests continued to aggressively demand an order of crucifixion. The hesitation on Pilate's face was evidence of an apparent inner turmoil. The mob began to grow restless. They chanted "Crucify him, crucify him," over and over again. The Roman guards were forcibly holding back the crowd from pressing onto the staircase. After a few moments of observation, Pilate succumbed to the pressure of the multitude. He again addressed the crowd, raising his hand to silence them long enough to shout, "He is to be flogged!"

The chief priest Annas appeared visibly agitated, but he did not protest. His cohorts, including his son-in-law Caiaphas, all grumbled among themselves, and I recall taking note of how bright and white their priestly garb looked in contrast to the gray of the stone pillars and the grit of the mob. Outwardly, they could be described as spotless, the picture of reverence, even pure – but the hatred in their faces and the malice in their words turned my stomach. All my life I had been taught to believe that the priests were undefiled. I was taught to modify my behavior to suit their ways because they appeared holier than I could ever be. But looking on, it seemed to me that outward purity was good for nothing, a farce, if the inward man was dark and corrupt.

Two of the nearby guards forcibly grabbed Jesus by the arms. His body lurched as they pulled him toward the staircase. Another guard fell in behind the trio as they descended the stairs. The crowd parted like a field of wheat as the guards led Jesus toward the square where public punishments were often carried out. As they passed, I was struck by the countenance of the guard in back. He appeared somehow apprehensive. His eyes met mine as they passed and, based on his gaze, I would not have been surprised had he run away like a startled hare. Pontius Pilate turned his back on the crowd and began to walk away. I could tell by his gait that he wanted nothing more to do with The King of the Jews.

Droves of people pressed into the small square to witness the flogging of Jesus of Nazareth. Only a fraction of the people from the courtyard would be able to fit, so people pressed and wriggled against one another like fish in a net. I was embroiled in outrage as I watched members of the crowd spit on him. Some of them hurled small stones as the guards pushed him forward. I could see tears welling in Peter's eyes as he pressed ahead of me into the square. He kept his face covered, but this time, he led the way, emboldened by his nearness to Christ and moved by his inability to help him.

Once inside the square, there was scarcely room to breathe. I was relieved the women had remained in the courtyard. The hoard was pressing into itself like a herd of cattle that had outgrown its pen. The movement of one person unsettled at least ten others. I did my best to press onward. I heard another woman in the crowd cry out, "Here is his follower!" as she pointed at John. Somehow, his face covering had been pulled away. He ignored her and hurried to cover himself. I looked to Peter for wisdom, fearful that the crowd may turn on him as well.

"James," Peter cried out. "James!"

"Sir, James is not with us," I yelled back, shaking my head. "He stayed on the rooftop!" I thought perhaps he meant to call John's name, and given the chaos of the experience, his mistake seemed plausible.

"No," Peter was merely inches from my ear as he yelled, but even so, I struggled to hear him over the crowd. "James, his brother!" He pointed toward the other man in our group. The man standing by John was preoccupied with a robust gentleman to his right who seemed to be out of sorts. They appeared to be in some form of an argument. It took me a moment to process what Peter was saying. When I finally understood that the other man was also called James, and that this James was the brother of Jesus, I nodded to Peter and pushed my way past the crowd to reach him.

"Sir, Peter has need of your attention! I yelled to combat the voice of the screaming man next to him. James, the brother of Jesus, left me holding his place as he pushed back toward Peter. The robust man pressed his round belly into me and laughed. I did my best to hold my ground. I steadied my footing and tensed my legs. It didn't take long to understand why James had been arguing with the man. He was rude. He wore a dusty robe and he sprayed spittle from his lips with every word he spoke. He smelled so much like a wet goat that I had to hold my breath for a moment. As more and more people pushed in around me, it became apparent that his was not the only ripe body in the crowd. As he forced his body into me once again, I saw James and John using their mass to create a space at the rail in front of them. We had managed to press as closely to the square as one could get without passing beyond the barrier.

Just as I found my footing next to Peter, the line of priests and scribes filed in to the loft at the back of the square. A handful of the Roman guard were gathered by a wooden table, covered with a woven cloth. The two guards flanking Jesus pushed him to the middle of the square. The crowd began to settle and the yelling and shoving subsided as the praetor signalled the guards to begin. We all watched as the Christ was bound to a whipping post in the center of the square. Then, one of the soldiers from the group by the table approached Jesus from behind. He laid hold of Jesus' robe just at the base of his neck and jerked it, causing it to pull violently against Jesus' throat. The guard pulled a knife from the leather sheath on his hip and gave it a quick but forceful yank through the upper part of the robe. He then returned the knife to its place and used his bare hands to rip the garment from Jesus' body, tearing it away from his skin with much more force than the task required. Reflexively, I turned my eyes away. To see him there, his body laid bare, was in and of itself difficult to take. But when the men removed the woven cloth from the table, I could no longer avert my eyes.

Another of the five guards retrieved a nine-tailed whip from the table, a flagellum, with what looked to be sharpened lead tips woven into its tails. His companions hung the woven cloth on a rack near to the table. At this point, even the murmuring in the crowd had ceased. I watched Peter's face intently. His lips moved as if he was speaking, but he was looking into the sky. The sight of him confused me, but then I saw a tear form at the corner of his eye and roll down his cheek before it became one with the drape that covered his face. I looked away from Peter and back to Jesus just as the praetor signaled the guard to begin.

The guard made no pretence of his duty, as he raised his strong arm and hurled his whip toward Christ with the force of an army. Jesus cried out as the free ends of the whip cut into his flesh. The soldier then pulled back with a mighty yank, and I watched as the blood sprayed across the square and as the meat was ripped from Christ's torso about his ribs. The shock of it stunned me. I almost lost my footing, but I didn't have time to steady myself before the next blow came, and then another and another. At one point, Peter and John were weeping so silently, yet so bitterly, that I myself felt tears forming in my eyes.

The soldiers whipped him and scourged him again and again, until the flesh hung from his body in large, loose strips. The meat from his body hung in gaping shreds, enough to expose the sinew and bone underneath. When one of the tails took a wild flight and wrapped around his head, it was all I could do to keep my stomach. As the guard yanked the whip back, the lead spike tore through Jesus' forehead, across the bridge of his nose and down his cheek like a jagged knife through warm butter. One of the women in the crowd screamed, and I watched as many people turned away. Even some of the priests could bear no more. I watched them turn their backs as a piece of loose and bloody meat flew hard against the woven cloth, now heavy with blood and flesh. Peter steadied himself against the railing. I could tell his strength was failing him. He cried out, "My Lord!" Several people in the crowd turned to look at him. John seemed ready to chastise him for risking their safety, but he stopped short when he saw the anguish in Peter's eyes.

Jesus fell to his knees as yet another crack of the whip tore flesh from the backs of his legs and backside. My face grew hot as my stomach churned within me once again. I held my breath. Surely this would be enough to satisfy the priests. Surely they would demand no more. The praetor raised his hand, signalling the soldier to stop. Jesus hung to the whipping post with his knees bent beneath him. Had I not known it was Jesus before me, had I not seen it with my own eyes, I would not have believed him to be a man. He didn't look human. The flesh hung from his body like tassels, dripping with blood. The two guards who had first escorted him returned and took him by the arms. They unshackled him from the post and pulled him to his feet. His legs were unsteady beneath him as they dragged him toward the collection of holding cells that bordered along the square. Was he to be imprisoned? What more could they possibly want from him?

I found myself transfixed by the sheer depth of the blood that pooled at the foot of the post. The ground was slick with crimson. Peter, John, and Jesus' brother James each held onto the railing as though it were the only thing keeping them from collapsing. The crowd began to thin as the guards removed Jesus from the square, and we all stood, silent, until the doors of the jailhouse slammed shut.

Without a word, John turned his back to us and moved quickly around the edge of the square. We watched as he spoke with a man opposite us along the rail. I didn't know the man, and from the look on Peter's face, nor did he. Jesus' brother held the railing with both hands, his head hung low between his arms. I couldn't tell if he was weeping, or if he thought he might be ill, or both. Just as I was about to reach out to him, John returned. "When they're finished with him, they'll return him to Pilate. We should make our way back to the courtyard."

We walked in silence. I looked toward the sun. So much had happened since dawn, and it couldn't have been more than eight o'clock, perhaps half past. I could feel the exhaustion of the day's events building in my bones. I wondered how I would ever return to my normal life after this day – how would I be able to move on? Once we were back inside the courtyard, we found that much of the crowd had, at least for a while, dispersed. We found Mary and Jesus' mother exactly where we'd left them, holding one another and weeping bitterly. They looked as though their tears had been flowing freely since the moment we departed. James gently touched Mary's shoulder and reached down to console his mother. He held her close to him, and she buried her face in his tunic and cried out. The pain in her voice was so agonizing I felt as though my own heart may shatter.

Soon the courtyard began to fill with people once again, and we needed no one to tell us that the guards were returning with Jesus. Mary stood to her feet and steadied herself. James held his mother as she prepared herself to see her son's battered body. I expected the guards to drag him into the courtyard through the crowd, but they did not. Instead, they must have taken a different path.

Pilate stepped out onto the platform at the top of the stairs and raised a hand to hush the crowd. The chief priests were all gathered, once again, at the front of the stairs beyond the crowd. "Again, I say to you, I have found no cause in this man, and yet to meet your demands, I have ordered him punished. Now I say to you, here is the man."

Two guards pushed Jesus out onto the platform. He shuffled forward, shackled at the ankles and at the wrists. In a cruel attempt at humiliation, the soldiers had fashioned what looked to be a ring of thorns and forced it onto his brow like a crown and draped him in a purple robe. His body was so badly beaten and covered in blood that even his own mother could not recognize him. "No!" she cried out, clutching her hand to her heart. I could tell that even Pilate was pained by what he saw. Perhaps the flogging had been worse than he expected. The multitude gasped at the sight of him. Some shielded their eyes.

One of the guards in front shouted, "All hail, King of the Jews," and laughter erupted among his ranks. But the priests and Pharisees were not amused. The soldier's words sent them into a fit of rage.

"Crucify, crucify!" they cried in unison. I stood in disbelief. This man was not a threat. He was a far cry from Cesar. I wanted to cry out my opposition, but I was consumed by fear. "Crucify him!" they shouted again.

"Shall I truly crucify your king?" Pilate asked, his voice thick with sarcasm and disdain. It was obvious to all that he had no desire to put Jesus to death.

The chief priest answered back, "We have no king but Cesar, and if you let this man live, you are no friend to our king." Pilate paced back and forth for a moment. The priests seized advantage of the time by shouting and flailing about, throwing stones and stirring the crowd into an uproar. The look on Pilate's face told an unsung truth, he feared an uprising. He stormed to the center of the platform and motioned for his aid to come near. The priests hushed the crowd and turned back to Pilate. "What say you?" the chief among them asked.

Pilate then turned to Jesus and spoke to him. I could not make out his words. The look on Pilate's face was pitiable, but he looked back to the crowd who stood at the ready to riot. Immediately, the aid returned with a pitcher. "I say, I wash my hands of this!" Pilate answered back to the priests. "I am innocent of this man's blood – if you want him dead, take him and crucify him, but his blood is on your hands!" Pilate's aid poured water over his hands, and we all watched as Pilate physically enacted his inward resolve.

The mother of Jesus collapsed to her knees on the ground near where I stood. Mary began to weep. I looked toward the men and watched the tears forming in all their eyes. Deep within, I knew I would be forever changed by all I had witnessed. I heard one of the priests cry out again, "His blood is on our heads and the heads of our children!" And with that, Pilate shook the excess water from his hands and turned his back on the crowd, and on Jesus, as the guards pushed him forward into the courtyard and drug him through the crowd, back toward the square.

Peter moved to follow, but a company of guards halted us and forced us back. I looked around to see guards clearing the courtyard all around us. "Golgotha!" the guard yelled, as if to tell us the route we should follow to witness the crucifixion. I looked to Peter. What would we do now? What could we do?

Peter stood for a moment, seemingly uncertain of what to do next. "What now?" John asked.

"I don't know," Peter answered.

"Well, we better decide quickly before the guards decide for us!" John returned.

"Let's clear the courtyard and then decide where to go," Peter suggested.

Outside the courtyard, we decided that we would follow Jesus along the path, in the hopes that we could somehow bring him comfort, or spare him, or help him in some way. I wondered if now would be the time for fighting – I hoped the answer would be no. "I will go and tell the others and meet you on the path!" John announced his intent and rushed off toward the rooftop. I imagined the group of men waiting there, uncertain, broken, or perhaps enraged. How must this scene have looked from a distance?

Peter led the way toward the road outside the square. We all followed behind. There were people everywhere. Everything about the day felt different, even the way people moved in the streets. We hadn't waited at the square for very long before we saw solders laying two notched Dogwood beams one over the other to form a cross in the road. I had never cared to see a cross up close, and being this close to one made my skin crawl. As the soldiers dropped it onto the ground, a cloud of dust flew into the air so thickly that I could no longer see my companions. As the dust settled, the main gate of the square opened and we saw Jesus, unshackled, but flanked by guards. One guard hit him with a rod to keep him moving, and I could tell by the way the other guards stood watching that they would make him carry his own cross.

Throngs of people gathered around him. They yelled and said hateful things. They spit on him and threw stones. When a small boy next to me lifted his arm to throw a small rock, I couldn't help myself and I grabbed his wrist to stop him. He looked at me with confusion, but the look on my face must have been easily read, because he dropped the stone and ran away – no doubt to tell his father. Regardless, I did not regret my choice.

The masses watched as Jesus struggled to hoist the large cross onto his shoulder. He appeared to be talking to himself occasionally and, at first, I wondered if he'd lost too much blood. I didn't understand it, but I remembered that I had seen both Peter and John talking to themselves throughout the morning. Was this practice typical for holy men?

I pushed the thought from my mind as I considered just how brutal the walk to Golgotha would be, especially under the load of a cross. I longed to help him, but the guards held us all back, no one could get near. As we neared a turn in the road, the crowd pressed in behind me. I found myself near enough to reach out and touch him. The guards were behind him and I thought I may have just enough time. I stretched out my hand toward the cross. "I am here. Do you know me?" I formed the thought in my mind, but I spoke not a word. I strained forward against the crowd and felt my fingertips graze the wood. I cannot explain what happened next in words. It is impossible to relay without sounding as though I'd succumbed to madness, and yet it was more real to me than even the ground beneath my feet. He saw me. He looked right into my eyes, and I heard his voice. He answered me, but he did not open his lips. He made no words with his mouth, and yet I heard his voice and I knew it was him. It was only three words, *I know you*, but somehow, I knew they would become the most important words I'd ever hear. But how? Why? I could not discern.

We made yet another turn and I could no longer see Peter or the others in the crowd. I'd lost them somewhere along the way. As I scanned the sea of faces for them, I realized that we were crossing the same road on which palm fronds had been laid at Jesus' feet just days ago. My heart sank. How fickle mankind could be. Whom could a man trust?

About that time, I saw James, the brother of Jesus, across the way, climbing a set of stairs with Mary and the mother of Jesus close behind him. I tried to look beyond them. It appeared they were looking for a place to get near to the cross. Inside my spirit, I willed the crowd to let them through. I wanted them to be near the cross almost as badly as I wanted to be there myself. Out of the corner of my eye, I saw someone strike one of the guards. I don't know who it was, but it certainly got the guards' attention, because they all turned on him. As they did so, a woman ahead of the cross took the opportunity to run to Jesus. She took the free end of her veil and blotted his face with it, and then she offered him a drink from a craft of water. She turned the cup up to his lips and, as the loud crack of a whip sounded behind me, she moved away from him and back into the crowd. Who was this woman? How many lives in this crowd had been changed by this man?

I saw the mother of Jesus pushing her way through a mob to the edge of the road, James and Mary right behind her. They were so close. The mother of Jesus called out to him, reaching her arm into the street as far as she could. I quickly turned to see if the nearby guard was watching. He was. I felt my chest tighten. I contemplated my next action. I had no desire to be arrested, and yet, I plotted. But, despite my readiness, the guard did nothing. I wondered if he knew of the family. I wondered if maybe he felt torn over the condemnation of an innocent man, or even if, maybe, he considered his own mother. Then again, I also thought maybe he was simply lazy and disinterested in his work.

Nonetheless, I turned back to his mother. As she stretched her hand forth, struggling to reach him, I saw his hand, shaking and dark with blood, slowly reach out in return. His fingers made contact with hers and they lingered for just a moment. She closed her fingertips around his hand as best she could until the crack of the whip forced him to move again. I didn't even realize I was crying until a man to my left asked me, "Is he your rabbi?"

"No," I replied as I turned away – but as soon as the word escaped my lips, it felt like a lie.

As we neared the steep rise to the hill called Golgotha, Jesus had reached a point of weakness so intense that the cross drug along the ground mere inches at a time. One of the guards shouted at him repeatedly to move faster as he beat him with a rod. I couldn't comprehend how the guard expected his efforts to be effective. What man ever gained strength from a beating? I was too afraid to speak my mind, but I wanted to yell out and draw attention to his ignorance. I felt rage growing in my spirit as I watched the sun reflect off the droplets of spit and sweat spraying into the air around the guard's pompous mouth. I was disgusted by him and could taste the sour bile of my own stomach in the back of my throat.

I lifted my eyes and looked around for Peter and the others, but I couldn't find them in the crowd. The closer we drew to the summit, the thicker the crowd became. A large number of Jesus' followers had gathered at the base of the hill to join him on the climb. Many were weeping and crying out, begging for his life to be spared. It was a strange and striking contrast to witness one man's hatred for Jesus, and mere inches away, another man's love for him. Had I met these people on the street, the look of them would never have told me such a story – I supposed it really was true that only God could see the heart of a man, and it was left to us to judge nothing more than that man's actions.

Jesus took one ragged and unsure step onto the steep part of the hill and fell hard against the rock, collapsing under the weight of the cross and, I imagined, under the weight of his immense burden. The cross came down hard upon his head and across his back, pushing the crown of thorns so deeply into his scalp that there would be no hope of dislodging it. I averted my eyes in reflex just as the guard used his rod to strike the long beam of the cross. He berated Christ, demanding that he rise and finish the walk. Jesus tried. He struggled against the weight of the crossbeam, crying out in effort, but try as he might, he could not move it.

The centurion of the Roman guard, who had followed the procession on horseback, called out loudly to a man walking beside the road in the direction of the market. I deduced the guard chose this man simply because he appeared to be the only man on the road who had no interest in the scene unfolding before him. From the look of him, he appeared to be a man of Cyrene, but I could not be certain. When the man attempted to keep walking on his way, another of the guards laid hold of him and turned him back toward the centurion on horseback. From behind them, surrounded by the mob, I could not make out the words that were spoken, but the time for talking ended quickly and the guards pushed the man toward the cross where it lay in the dust. To everyone's shock, the man reached down and turned the crossbeam into the air, placing his shoulder into the crux where the two beams met. He shored his footing and squared his shoulders toward the hill. Jesus climbed slowly from his knees and clung to the cross as he steadied himself. He squeezed the wood with his fingertips, driving his fingernails into the grain with all the strength he had left to muster and then turned toward the hill again. Together they began the slow ascent to the Place of the Skull, Jesus walking slightly ahead of the Cyrenian.

At the top of the hill, the sun reflected off the rocks in such a way that it caused my eyes to squint. There was so much shouting and jeering and, at the same time, wailing and crying out that I could not understand any of the words spoken by those around me. Golgotha could be seen from almost any place inside the city walls, and I wondered if the other men were still on the rooftop, or if they had braved the ascent and now stood somewhere in the crowd. I looked for Peter and John, and even for Mary, in the sea of faces on the hill, but I could not find them – though I somehow knew they were there. I looked up toward the sky to gauge the position of the sun. It must have been closing in on nine o'clock. For a moment, my family entered my mind. They would be looking for me by now. How would I explain myself? But then, two guards drug Jesus to the cross and laid him across it. As I watched his shredded flesh rake across the grain of the wood, I felt the dagger of guilt pierce my heart. How could I consider myself in any way? How could my small problems or worry over my wife's chastising hold even a moment of my attention when compared to the agony of this Galilean – this Messiah?

As I wrestled with my guilt, I watched the guards tether Jesus to the cross. And then, I could not help but hold my breath as one of the praetor's men held a mallet high above his head and drove it downward against an iron spike. The sound of the hammer against the spike set my teeth on edge. The spike passed through Jesus' hand as blood sprayed in all directions. I saw a man across from me become ill, right there in the dirt. I couldn't be certain, but he had the look of a man I'd seen many times begging by the pool at Siloam. But it could not have been that man, because that man had been born blind and this was assuredly a sighted man.

The blood that poured from Jesus' wound looked dark and thick, almost like honey dripping from the comb. The praetor's men repeated the gruesome task again on his left hand, and I averted my eyes. When they moved to his feet, they affixed a small block of wood into place against the beam that would force Jesus to keep his knees bent as he hung on the cross, preventing him from finding relief in even the slightest form. The two soldiers came down hard with their hammers and drove large spikes through his feet and into the wood. The sound the deed made was deafening. But as they worked, the sound of Jesus' voice could be heard over the multitude as he cried out in a loud voice, "Abba!" The priests were aghast at his use of the word. He cried out to God like a small child crying out for his father. His vernacular tested me. I had long been taught that such a thing was irreverence and blasphemous, and though my ears bristled at first, my heart cried out from within me to tell me the truth of who Jesus was. Once he was secure, the guards gathered around something on the ground. One knelt down and the others stood and laughed as they watched him. After a moment, they carried what looked like a piece of thin birch over to the cross and laid it on the beam above Jesus' head. After it had been nailed into place, I struggled to make it out but could not read it from my distance.

Then, a team of guards hoisted the cross into the air. Blood ran over the cross like oil. Some in the crowd jeered and others fell silent as the soldiers let the long end of the structure fall into a hole that would hold it erect. I felt physical pain tear through my body as the force of the fall thrust Jesus' body against the spikes and tethers. My pain, coupled with the brokenness in my spirit, forced me to my knees as I watched. From my position, I looked up to see the sign the guards had affixed above Jesus' head. It read, *Jesus of Nazareth, King of the Jews*.

Jesus cried out in aguish as the cross fell into place. The soldiers continued to mock him and prod him as he hung. At one point, instead of water to quench his thirst, they pressed a sponge soaked in vinegar against his bloodied lips. I could see how it burned his raw flesh by the grimace in his eyes. In his agony, he looked up to the sky and prayed aloud, "Father, forgive them, for they know not what they do!" I wanted to tear my clothes! How could this man pray for those who hurt him so willingly? My inability to comprehend it threatened to drive me mad! I could see a look of disbelief wash over the chief priests' faces. Another of the scribes began to shake at the knees. He appeared to be full of fear, or guilt, or both.

Until that very moment, I had not noticed that two other men had also been hung on the hill that day, one on either side of Jesus. The guards hoisted Christ up between the two men who, I later learned, had been sentenced to death as thieves. I looked to the sky again. In just a few short hours, I'd gone from a simple stroll under the stars to standing on Golgotha with a group of wanted men, whilst watching the crucifixion of a rabbi who may very well be the Messiah. What a morning this had become.

For a long while, Jesus simply hung there on the cross, writhing, struggling to breath and fighting his pain. A crowd of his followers had remained on the hill for hours, as did a collection of guards, the chief priests and scribes, and a spattering of common folk who believed him to be a blasphemer. I saw Peter in the crowd. He had moved away from the others and stood alone, as close to the foot of the cross as the guards would allow. Mary and the mother of Jesus had positioned themselves directly in front of him. I do not think they took their eyes off him even for a moment. The soldiers, perhaps out of boredom, or perhaps out of a ploy to later gain a profit, began to cast lots for Jesus' clothing. They laughed and joked, entertaining themselves. They seemed to give little regard to the three men barely clinging to life on the hill.

More of the crowd began to disperse as the hours waned, but I could not tear myself away. As the morning dwindled, one of the thieves cried out in anguish. He gnashed his teeth together and threw his head back. His mop of black hair hung wildly down his back against his cross. He then lashed out at Jesus in anger, shouting that if Jesus were truly the Chosen One, he would free them all from the cross. The thief who had been hung on the other side of Jesus shouted back at him in return, "Let him alone! He is an innocent man!" I remember being taken aback by the second thief's face. It was almost childlike, sweet. Not at all what one would expect from a thief. Again, I marveled at how the look of a man and the heart of him could be so vastly different. The second thief continued, "He's done nothing wrong! We are but getting what we deserve!" Then this same thief turned his eyes toward Jesus and said, "Remember me when you come into your Kingdom."

I covered my mouth in awe. The priests and scribes were clearly agitated by the thief's words. The crowds of people who remained on the hill reacted in many various ways. So divided was the multitude, that I was surprised no fighting had begun. Jesus could barely move, but he turned his face toward the man and answered, "Today, you will be with me in Paradise." I was so struck by those words that I am sure my mouth hung open in a gape. How such beautiful and caring words could fall from a mouth so badly beaten was beyond my greatest comprehension. The camp of priests erupted in anger and agitation, tearing at their robes and making a show of their discontent, grumbling amongst themselves.

My legs had grown so tired, I could no longer stand. I looked to the sky once again. The sun was almost directly overhead when a hard wind began to blow. Without warning, darkness fell over the land as though the sun had been blotted from the sky. The people around me grew terrified. Some of the priests fled and many of the onlookers abandoned their places on the hill and ran back to their homes in an attempt to escape the mystery of the darkness. I could tell some of the priests had begun to doubt their own righteousness, while others stood proud. In the darkness, I crawled over to the place where Peter knelt. I placed a hand on his shoulder and I could sense his grief and his confusion. He didn't say so, but it seemed to me that he expected Jesus to prove his might that very day, to overthrow the Romans and the Pharisees and take his rightful place as King. But just then, I heard the Christ call out from the cross, "My God, my God, why have you forsaken me?" and it became painfully clear to me that Jesus would not walk away from the cross in triumph.

It seemed as though hours had passed as we remained gathered there in the darkness. I could no longer tell the time because the sun gave no light. The high wind had been blowing steadily since the darkness fell and I clutched my tunic to my body for added warmth. Some of the guards held torches that did a wild dance in the wind, but cast just enough light to illuminate the agony on the hill. We could see that Jesus' breath was slowing. I could no longer hold back my tears as we all watched him gasping for air like a fish writhing on dry land. As I watched him, there beside Peter in the dirt on the hill called Golgotha, he spoke again, "Father, into your hands I commit my spirit. It is finished." With that, he gave up the ghost and died.

As soon as his head dropped low against his chest, the earth beneath us began to quake. Panic set in among the people. His followers mourned with great sorrow, crying out in loud voices, but they did not flee, despite the fearsome nature of the wind and darkness. With that, the shaking of the earth grew stronger and the heavy veil of the temple tore in two from bottom to top! I gasped in disbelief. No one had touched it, no one was near to it. Not even the strongest man in Jerusalem could have accomplished such a feat. I could see the whites of the chief priests' eyes as they grew wide and fearful. The soldiers charged with guarding Jesus were uneasy. One ran away furiously as the earth quaked beneath his feet. He fled down the hill and toppled as he ran, rolling end over end in the shadow of darkness. As more people fled in fear, the centurion did his best to steady his horse. As he did so, he called out in the direction of the Pharisees, "Surely this was the Son of God!" He yelled with such guttural authority that another guard dropped his spear and knelt on the spot, weeping as though his life had just been stripped from him. The baltea of his uniform made a clinking sound as it whipped in the wind. How would he live with himself after this day? The centurion called out to the now lone guard remaining at the cross and signaled him to spear Jesus, to guarantee his death. The guard held the spear in his hand and thrust it upward into Jesus' side. Blood and water poured from the wound like a spring in the desert.

Mary, James, and his mother had moved near to the foot of the cross. No guard stood by to stop them. None would dare try. The women wept and cried out. Peter and I moved closer to them. As I stood there staring up at the cross where Jesus' lifeless body hung limp against the wood, the reality of what I had just witnessed began to set in. I took note of the darkened sky, the earthquake, the torn veil at the temple and my heart began to beat rapidly in my chest. I was overcome with fear and

I fled. God help me, I fled. I ran as fast as I could down the hill, stumbling and tripping in the darkness. I am ashamed to admit it now, but in that moment, the fear was too much to bear – it was impossible to run from the fear, but I tried. I ran as hard and as fast as I could, back to my own street and my own house.

But instead of turning to my own front door, for reasons I still don't fully understand, I kept running. I passed my home and returned to the small house where I had first been introduced to followers of the rabbi Jesus. There was only one man inside the house, the man who had told us of Judas' demise. He had a ruddy complexion and his tunic was dusted with flour. I could tell he had been at the millstone as he dusted his hands on the rag he had tied over his belt. I could smell stew in the air and I wondered if any of the others would have the stomach for an evening meal. He recognized my face, though I did not know his name, nor he mine. He appeared to be busying himself for the sake of being busy, perhaps in an effort to quiet his troubled mind. He appeared to be going about the preparation for the Sabbath day. My mind reeled, and I could tell this man understood my plight. He offered me some warm bread and wine, and I eagerly accepted. I wasn't hungry in the slightest, but I thought perhaps the food would do me some good. Perhaps it would right my mind. I found a place on the floor by the fire and lounged in silence as the man went about his work, only stopping to wipe his tears or look out into the street. I assumed he was watching for the others or for approaching members of the Roman guard. I opened my mouth to offer help, and though my will was intact, the physical ability to stand had escaped me. He told me to rest, and I was grateful.

After I had my bread and wine, I felt the exhaustion of the day closing in on me. My eyes grew heavy and, though I fought to stay awake, my body wouldn't allow it and I fell asleep. I have no idea how long I laid there on the floor, for I have no idea what time it was when I arrived back at the house. Instead, I was startled awake the next morning by the sound of movement in the room. One man tiptoed toward the door and several others lay sleeping. The man who had startled me let the door close quietly behind him. I assumed he was taking a trip to the latrine and I knew I would not be far behind him. Not every man was there, but I did see Peter, who was leaning upright against a wall, as though sleep had come against his will as well.

As the sun rose on the Sabbath, so did the atmosphere of grief. Several of the men had watched as members of the Roman guard sealed Jesus' tomb with a large rock. They shared that two men by the names of Nicodemus and Joseph had taken Jesus' body off the cross and prepared the grave clothes with

Myrrh and spices and then carried him into the tomb. I could not help but think about his mother. I wondered if she had seen the tomb sealed and my heart broke for her. Having recently lost my own mother to sickness intensified my pain.

There was so much confusion in the house that day, about what had transpired and what to expect next, that I feared to question anyone. I could tell the men didn't know what to do. Some discussed returning to their previous lives and picking up where they'd left off, not out of desire, but out of a lack of options. On the one hand, they seemed crushed that Jesus didn't come down off the cross and assert himself as king, and on the other hand, they tried to remain faithful to the promises he had made them. They clung to their hope by a single strand of hair. It seemed evident to me that they had truly believed Jesus would conquer Jerusalem and become king. They had been committed to him, and now he was gone. His death also meant death to their way of life.

The morning gave way to afternoon on that silent Saturday, and I finally mustered the courage to ask Peter to tell me more about Jesus. He hesitated, still grief stricken and confused, but he began to share with me some of the things he'd seen and done since meeting the rabbi. As he spoke, some of the other men began to share as well. I listened to story after story and heard the men tell of miracle after miracle. Hours passed, and I found myself so riveted by the accounts of Jesus that I mourned the loss of a relationship that could now never be.

An urgent knock came at the gate just as we were placing food on the table for the Sabbath supper. The men in the room tensed. I realized at once that we had let our guards down. Peter was the first to stand and Matthew after him. James drew a poker from the fire and, with his action, I felt my heart move into my throat. "It is only Andrew!" Peter announced. Again, the relief in the room was palpable. How much more of this could I take? James ran to open the gate, still grasping the poker in his fist. Once inside, Andrew lowered the hood from his head and turned to the basin to clean his hands. "Where have you been, brother?" Peter threw his arms around Andrew, as though they had been parted for years.

"I snuck to the tomb, but there were guards in place!" Andrew answered. "The priests have gone so far as to have guards placed outside the tomb, imagine such a thing!" Peter looked from man to man. I couldn't tell if he full of hope, or fear.

As we sat to eat the evening meal of stew and bread, I thought of my family, eating their Sabbath meal without me, wondering where I must be. What must they think? Guilt threatened to consume me. But as Peter sat next to me, wiping tears from his eyes once again, my guilt melted away as he began to tell me about the Kingdom of God as he'd come to know it through Jesus' teachings. And somehow, I knew I was exactly where I was supposed to be.

Saturday was both long and short at the same time. Spending the day with men who were mourning the loss of their closest friend and teacher was difficult, perhaps the most difficult part of the whole experience. I mourned him too, especially having seen it all unfold. But my familiarity with Jesus had been from a distance. I had never known him like these men. Still, what had happened to me in the courtyard and then again on the road – those experiences were undeniable. Every time I started to doubt a story I heard from the men in the room, I could once again hear Jesus' voice saying "I know you." I told Peter I could not rationalize the things I'd heard. I could not make sense of it, no matter how hard I tried. He answered me by saying that Jesus had once told him "*All* things are possible for one who believes," and I marveled at his words.

As evening turned to night, the house grew quiet. Something about the darkness intensified the grief. Pain seems to become more acute at night. I should have gone to my own home, but I could not, and these men had now embraced me as one of their own. I felt a sense of purpose within this group unlike anything I'd ever felt before. It seemed as though simply being near them gave me something greater than myself to base my life around. I could not explain it. On this night, I was given a mat to sleep on in the upstairs room. Peter withdrew to an inner room by himself, feeling the need to be alone. But John sat and talked with me into the night. He asked me had I met Jesus before this day, would I have followed him, would I want to be a fisher of men, and even though I had no idea what he meant, something compelled me to say yes.

At some point, both John and I fell asleep, sitting upright on my borrowed mat, leaning against the wall. When day broke on the dawn after the Sabbath, rest had restored my sense of responsibility and I knew I simply had to go home. I imagined my wife moving from neighbor to neighbor asking for help to find me. I pictured my sons visiting the home of the physician on the far side of the city or visiting the prison. My heart ached and I longed to go to them. I chastised myself for being so captivated by this man Jesus that I would so easily neglect all that I held dear in my life, but at the same time, I could not deny that I felt no guilt or shame in my choice. My life had been forever changed by what I witnessed on that Friday, and by what I heard on that Sabbath Saturday – and now I found myself eager to discover what those things might mean for my Sunday. I could feel change deep in my heart – a form of excitement I couldn't explain, as though something wonderful had happened. But, when I looked around, nothing had changed. It was both exhilarating and agonizing at the same time.

I rose as quietly as I could, hoping I might be able to sneak away without waking the others, but as the morning sun began to wash the room in light through the only open window in the entire house, the others began to stir. I explained that I must go and tend to my family, and I thanked them all for their graciousness. I gave my word that I would return, and I embraced Peter as a brother. As I passed through the gate and onto the road home, I saw two women approaching. They were running and shouting and raising their arms into the air. As they grew closer, even from a ways off, I could see that it was Mary, along with the mother of Jesus. I moved to the side of the road to let them pass. They were moving so quickly, they didn't even see me. What had happened?

I turned again toward home, and then stopped in my tracks, turning back to the house where the disciples of Jesus had stayed. I stopped behind a stone wall and listened from a distance while Mary told Peter and John that they had been to the tomb and that the stone was rolled back. They spoke of an earthquake and of an angel who had the appearance of lightning who told them to share the good news! The guards had become so afraid that they fainted straightaway. Then, Mary said something that struck me to my core. "We have seen the Messiah! He lives!" she shouted out the words. "We fell at his feet! We touched him!" Mary held up her slender hands as though to emphasize the physical nature of her experience. I don't know why I kept myself hidden. I think it was because I felt somehow unworthy of these men. It doesn't make sense to me now, but watching the scene unfold from behind the stone wall felt right to me at the time. Could it be? Could he really live? Had he risen? Reason pushed doubt into my mind, but something in my heart forced me to push back. Yes! He had risen! I believed!

Peter shouted and the others ran to hear his words. There was much rejoicing at the gate as Mary and the mother of the Jesus turned to lead the men toward the tomb, so they could see the sight with their own eyes. They ran, and as they passed me, crouched in my hiding place behind the small stone wall, I heard Mary say, "Galilee! He said to tell his brothers that he would meet them in Galilee!"

I gathered myself and, as soon as they were out of sight, I ran as fast as I could toward my home. I ran down the street and past the place where, just days prior, I had met Peter in the dust, past the place I had concealed him in the shadows, past the place my life had changed forever without me even knowing. I burst through the door of my home and found my wife pacing. She had a broom in her grasp, but she wasn't at work. A look of worry was spread across her lovely face as she pulled her soft brown hair to one side. I was moved by my love for her and felt my eyes grow teary. When she turned to me, I could see a blend of relief and anger in her eyes, but I addressed neither. I grabbed her and pulled her close to me, kissing her a great many times. She began to laugh and seemed to forget her anger.

"What has happened?" she asked breathlessly.

"I must go again! I must go to Galilee!" I told her. "Tell my sons to meet me there!" I shouted as I rushed back toward the door. My excitement and anticipation seemed to have renewed my youth.

"Galilee?" my wife asked as she followed me outside, clearly confused. "What is in Galilee that our sons should travel two days to meet you there?"

"The Messiah!" I answered.

Look for the author's other works:

~Hangdog – Shoulder to Shoulder~
~Hangdog II – Rebirth~
~Hangdog III — The Absolution~

AUTHOR'S NOTE

Thus far in my life, I have yet to do anything one hundred percent flawlessly. This work is no exception. I have done my best to present accuracy and continuity in every line, but if you search for mistakes, you'll likely find them.

I should also add that this is a work of fiction. Names, characters, events and incidents are either the products of my imagination or used in a fictitious manner. Any resemblance to actual persons, living or dead, or actual events is purely coincidental.

WHAT I BELIEVE

As this is a work of *Christian* fiction, I would be remiss not to share the greatest news I've ever received – Christ. I believe in the One living God, and Jesus Christ as God in the flesh. I believe Christ died on the cross at the hands of sinful man to redeem me (all of us) from our sin and to restore our perfect relationship with the Father. I believe in *every* promise of Scripture. I believe in miracles – I've lived them. I believe God wants to bless us – I walk in it. I believe He wants us to live lives full of joy. I believe He wants the best for us. And I believe loving others means sharing this news, come what may.

THE PLAN OF SALVATION

Accepting this gift is simple – Once you've chosen to trust Christ as your Savior, and you truly believe in your heart that God loves you, that He sent His son, Jesus, to die as redemption for your sins, and that Christ rose again to conquer the grave, all you have to do is confess that belief.

"[9] If you declare with your mouth, "Jesus is Lord," and believe in your heart that God raised him from the dead, you will be saved. [10] For it is with your heart that you believe and are justified, and it is with your mouth that you profess your faith and are saved." Romans 10:9-10

Once you've done these things, it's time to live as a Christ follower. It's challenging, but it's the most amazing, rewarding adventure I've ever been on. Get into the Bible, find like-minded people, and take active steps to resist sin and to grow in your faith. Once you see what God has in store for your life, you, too, will want to shout it from the rooftops – I guarantee it.

www.ingramcontent.com/pod-product-compliance
Lightning Source LLC
Chambersburg PA
CBHW071212130626
46555CB00004B/1675